£ 5-95

CW00493602

Treble Recorder

Scales & Arpeggios

from 2018

ABRSM Grades 6-8

Contents

First published in 2017 by ABRSM (Publishing) Ltd, a wholly owned subsidiary of ABRSM
© 2017 by The Associated Board of the Royal Schools of Music
Unauthorized photocopying is illegal

Music origination by Julia Bovee
Cover by Kate Benjamin & Andy Potts
Printed in England by Page Bros (Norwich) Ltd, on materials from sustainable sources

Grade 6

SCALES

from memory
tongued *and* slurred

one octave and down to the dominant ♩ = 96

to a twelfth ♩ = 96

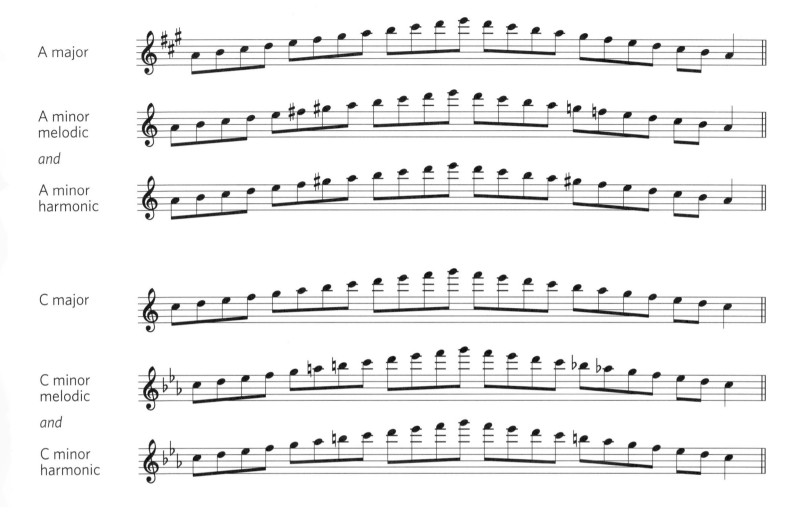

A major

A minor melodic

and

A minor harmonic

C major

C minor melodic

and

C minor harmonic

SCALE IN THIRDS

from memory
tongued *and* slurred

one octave ♩ = 88

F major

Grade 6

ARPEGGIOS

from memory
tongued *and* slurred

one octave and down to the dominant ♩. = 48

to a twelfth ♩. = 48

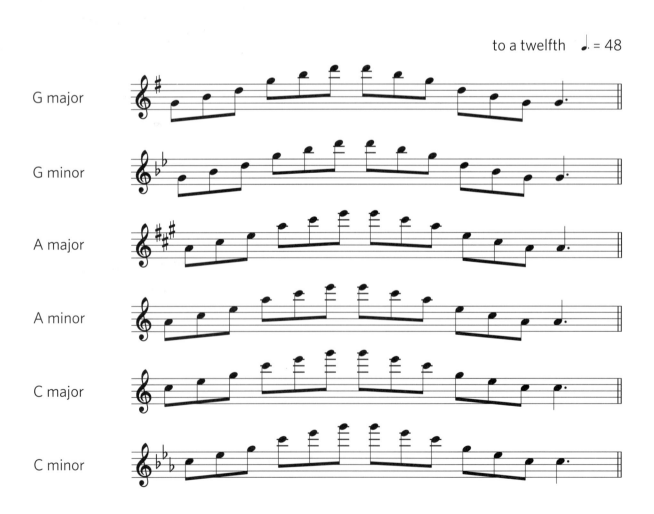

DOMINANT SEVENTHS

from memory
resolving on the tonic
tongued *and* slurred

Grade 6

DIMINISHED SEVENTHS

from memory
tongued *and* slurred

one octave ♩ = 72

starting
on B

starting
on C#

to a twelfth ♩ = 72

starting
on A

7

Grade 6

CHROMATIC SCALES

from memory
tongued *and* slurred

one octave ♩ = 96

starting on B

starting on C#

to a twelfth ♩ = 96

starting on A

8

Grade 7

SCALES

from memory
legato-tongued, staccato *and* slurred

one octave and down to the dominant ♩ = 112

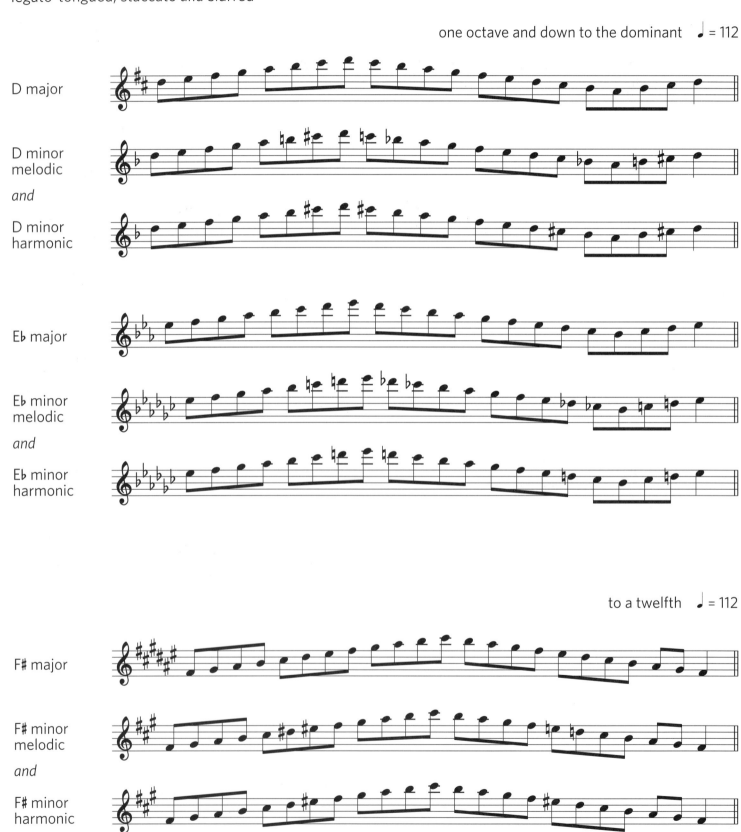

D major

D minor melodic

and

D minor harmonic

Eb major

Eb minor melodic

and

Eb minor harmonic

to a twelfth ♩ = 112

F# major

F# minor melodic

and

F# minor harmonic

G major

G minor
melodic

and

G minor
harmonic

Ab major

G# minor
melodic

and

G# minor
harmonic

EXTENDED-RANGE SCALE

from memory
legato-tongued, staccato *and* slurred

♩ = 112

Bb major

SCALE IN THIRDS

from memory
legato-tongued, staccato *and* slurred

one octave ♩ = 100

C major

Grade 7

ARPEGGIOS

from memory
legato-tongued, staccato *and* slurred

one octave and down to the dominant ♩. = 54

D major

D minor

E♭ major

E♭ minor

to a twelfth ♩. = 54

F♯ major

F♯ minor

G major

G minor

A♭ major

G♯ minor

DOMINANT SEVENTHS

from memory
resolving on the tonic
legato-tongued, staccato *and* slurred

Grade 7

DIMINISHED SEVENTHS

from memory
legato-tongued, staccato *and* slurred

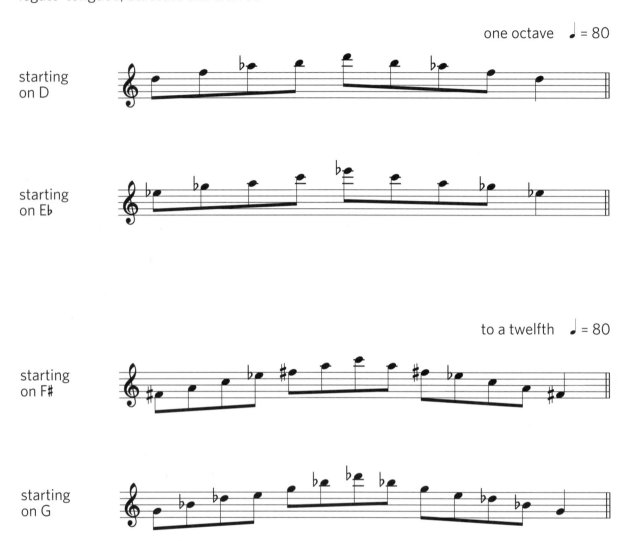

For practical purposes, the diminished sevenths are notated using some enharmonic equivalents.

CHROMATIC SCALES

from memory
legato-tongued, staccato *and* slurred

one octave ♩ = 112

starting on D

starting on E♭

to a twelfth ♩ = 112

starting on F#

starting on G

Grade 8

SCALES

from memory
legato-tongued, staccato *and* slurred

one octave and down to the dominant ♩ = 132

E major

E minor
melodic

and

E minor
harmonic

to a twelfth ♩ = 132

G# minor
melodic

and

G# minor
harmonic

A major

A minor
melodic

and

A minor
harmonic

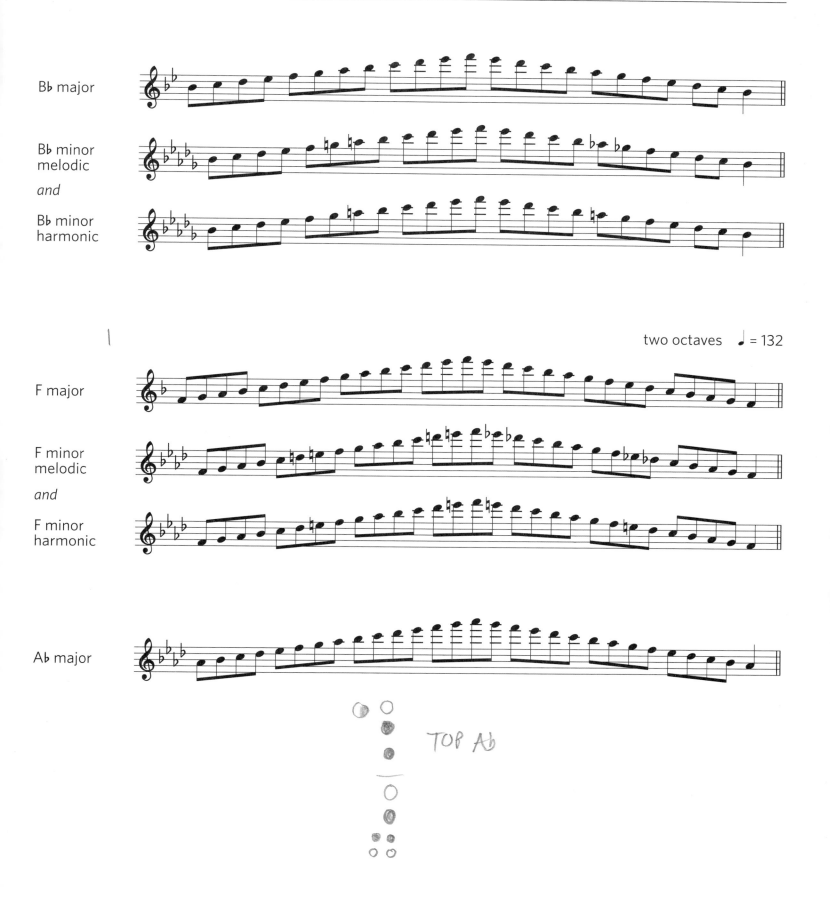

Grade 8

EXTENDED-RANGE SCALES

from memory
legato-tongued, staccato *and* slurred

♩ = 132

Eb major

D minor
harmonic

SCALES IN THIRDS

from memory
legato-tongued, staccato *and* slurred

one octave ♩ = 120

D major

to a twelfth ♩ = 120

G major

Grade 8

ARPEGGIOS

from memory
legato-tongued, staccato *and* slurred

one octave and down to the dominant   ♩. = 63

E major

E minor

to a twelfth   ♩. = 63

G♯ minor

A major

A minor

B♭ major

B♭ minor

two octaves   ♩. = 63

F major

F minor

A♭ major

EXTENDED-RANGE ARPEGGIOS

from memory
legato-tongued, staccato *and* slurred

E♭ major

D minor

Grade 8

DOMINANT SEVENTHS

from memory
resolving on the tonic
legato-tongued, staccato *and* slurred

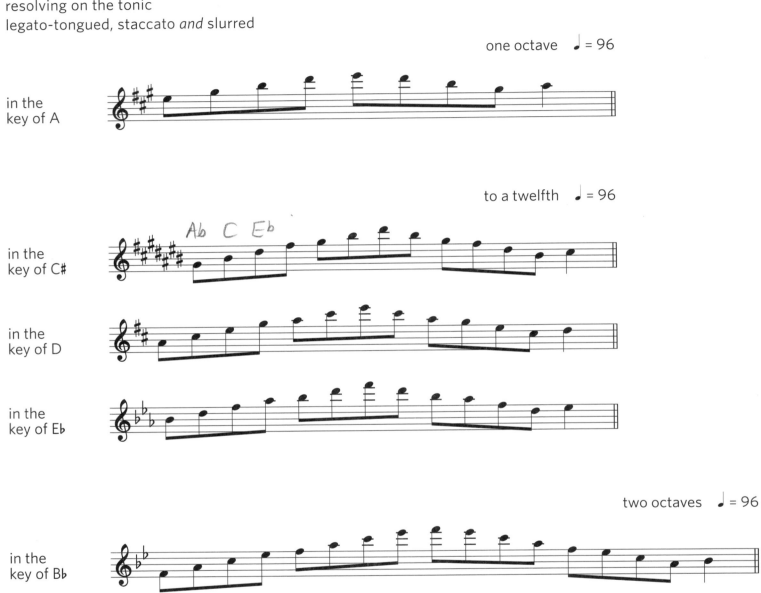

DIMINISHED SEVENTHS

from memory
legato-tongued, staccato *and* slurred

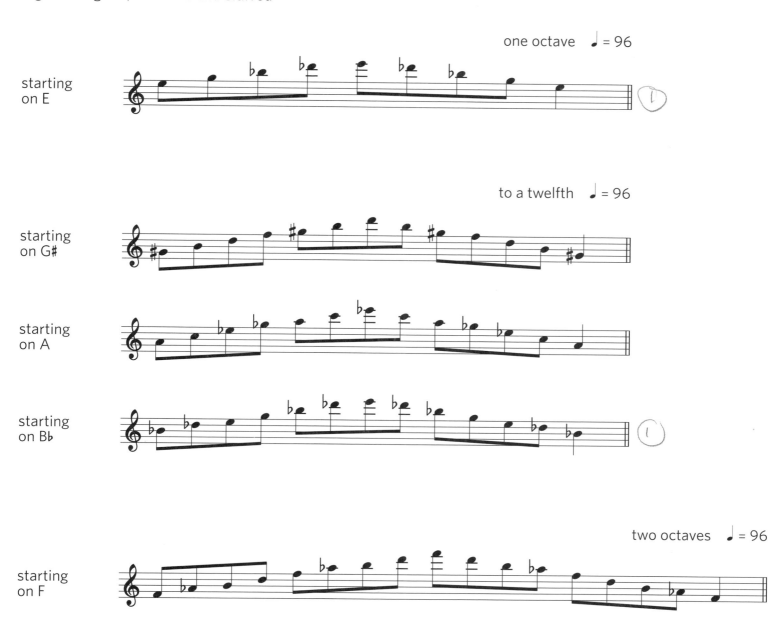

For practical purposes, the diminished sevenths are notated using some enharmonic equivalents.

Grade 8

CHROMATIC SCALES

from memory
legato-tongued, staccato *and* slurred

one octave ♩ = 132

starting
on E

to a twelfth ♩ = 132

starting
on G#

starting
on A

starting
on B♭

two octaves ♩ = 132

starting
on F

Grade 8

WHOLE-TONE SCALES

from memory
legato-tongued, staccato *and* slurred

one octave   ♩ = 132

starting
on D♭

two octaves   ♩ = 132

starting
on G